CINDERE

Reprinted 1996
First published 1995 by
WOLFHOUND PRESS
68 Mountjoy Square
Dublin 1

Wolfhound Press receives financial assistance from the Arts Council /
An Chomhairle Ealaíon, Dublin, Ireland

British Library Cataloguing-in-Publication Data
A catalogue record for this book is available from the British Library

ISBN 0-86327-493-5

Cover illustration: Marie-Louise Fitzpatrick
Cover design: Joe Gervin
Typesetting: Wolfhound Press
Printed in the UK by Cox & Wyman Ltd., Reading, Berks.

Also by Aislinn O'Loughlin
A Right Royal Pain (1996)
Shak and the Beanstalk (1997)

CINDERELLA'S FELLA

Aislinn O'Loughlin

Illustrated by

Marie-Louise Fitzpatrick

WOLFHOUND PRESS

To my brother, Seán,
who saved this book from computer
limbo more times than I can count

1

Hi! I'm Charming!

No! Don't laugh! It's my name.

Honest!

Well, okay, it's not actually my real name. It's my nickname. Sort of. You see, my mom died when I was only six years old, and for some reason my dad decided that Fred wasn't a very good name for me after all (my mom was the one who chose it in the first place).

Personally, I don't see anything wrong with it (not compared to Charming anyway) but he just reckoned it wasn't really right for a prince.

Oh yeah, I forgot to mention that bit, didn't I?

I'm a prince, soon to become king, and hating every minute of it. But anyway, as I was saying, while I thought Fred was a really nice name, my dad didn't.

Now, it just so happened that King Roland in the next kingdom had a son with a very princely

5

(and, in my opinion, cissy) name. He was called 'Charming', and, for reasons best known to him (you know what parents are like!) my dad decided that would be a very good name for me, and so I became 'Prince Fred the Charming' or as most people insist on calling me, 'Prince Charming'.

YUCK!!!!

Anyway, back to the story at hand. About a month before my eighteenth birthday my dad called me to the throne room. No, sorry, it was more like he sent for me to come to the throne room. Dad had never had that much time for me. Not since he remarried anyway.

So when Angelo (one of my two best friends) told me that my father 'requested my presence in the throne room promptly', I really was very surprised. Since when did my dad care about seeing me at all, never mind promptly!

But my good humour was soon crushed as I heard what Dad had to say. Not that it wasn't full of good intentions, mind you. In fact, it couldn't have been fuller. And that was the problem. Dad was over the moon with a great

idea which he'd had. The best birthday present in the world. A huge ball to be held on the eighteenth of July, on my birthday. Oh, sure, that sounds really great, doesn't it? But there was just one small, tiny, teensy weensy, microscopic catch. You see, this was not any old every day, ordinary ball that he was planning. This was to be the ball at which I was to choose my future wife.

That was it. I had basically no say in the matter. As far as he was concerned, it was just a case of 'Right, my charming son, next month you'll be eighteen. And here's what we'll do. I'll hold an absolutely huge ball for you, and you can invite all the young ladies of the kingdom to come. You'll dance with them all and the one you like best, you'll marry. Okay? Good! That's settled then. Now run along and play.' (Run along and play? At seventeen?)

And that was it.

No 'And what do you think of that idea, then?' or 'If that's okay by you, that is.'

Frankly, I really doubt if he could have cared less whether or not it was okay with me (which, by the way, it wasn't). As far as he was concerned, I'd go to the ball and marry one of those girls, whether I liked it or not!

Needless to say, the next month was a very busy one. The castle was in total and utter chaos. The poor cooks barely ever got out of the kitchen, and my stepmom even threw on an apron and went down to help them. Not a very queenly thing to do, my snobbish dad said, to which my stepmom, Sandra, replied that she was a kitchen girl by birth and she still enjoyed cooking. Sandra hates people telling her what to do.

I didn't hear the end of it from Matthew (my

other best friend) and Angelo. Matthew worked in the stables and Angelo was a messenger boy. All they ever did was complain about long hours, hard work, short breaks and low pay. I pointed out to them that they were working the same hours as usual with a higher wage, but it didn't seem to matter.

Not that I was much fun to be with either. I just sat about in the castle, saying that life wasn't fair, and also trying to figure out how I could either love someone I didn't know, or marry someone I didn't love. I couldn't come up with an answer to either question.

And my stepsisters, Grace and Belle, just moped around in their bedrooms all day because they were too young to go to the ball. That is, they moped around until Dad told them that they could have a slumber party with a few friends, and even take food from *my* party for it.

That put me in a right mood (I was being very selfish that month), until Sandra asked me if I'd rather have them watching my every move at the ball. I felt like telling her that the twins could have the whole thing for all I cared.

2

Finally, the eighteenth of July came. The whole castle, no, the whole kingdom was buzzing with excitement. I must have been the only person who wasn't excited. The ball was starting at nine o'clock that night, and by six o'clock, most people were indoors getting ready, or helping someone else to get ready. Angelo would be coming, with his cousin Maria, and Matthew was bringing a girl called Beth who lived near his house.

At seven o'clock, I started to get ready for the ball. First I put on my new suit, which Dad had got made specially for the ball. I hate getting measured for new suits, it's got to be the most boring thing in the world; and the stupid thing was that I still had a perfectly good suit which I had only worn once, in May, for the twins' eighth birthday party. What a waste of good linen.

Next I put some wax in my hair, to stop it

flopping into my eyes while I was dancing with Miss Perfect (though I still wasn't convinced she was coming). Then, checking myself in the mirror one last time, I grabbed my crown and put it carefully on top of my head.

By the time I was ready, it was only eight o'clock, so I had a full hour to waste before the ball started. I sat on my bed and wondered what to do for the next hour. Suddenly, it hit me. The twins! I'd hardly seen them at all in the past month, and I missed their friendly smiles and chatter.

'Hi, can I come in?' I asked, poking my head around the door of the spare dining room.

Belle and Grace were busy arranging jellies, cakes, cream buns, trifles and drinks on the table.

'Why not?' asked Belle, pushing her floppy blonde hair out of her eyes.

I stepped in and closed the door.

'Looking forward to your party tonight?' I asked, trying to think of something to say.

'Sure,' replied Grace, 'but I'll bet you're looking forward to your ball even more.'

I shook my head.

'I seriously doubt it,' I laughed.

Belle and Grace looked at each other. 'Why not?' asked Grace curiously.

I looked from one to the other.

'I just don't think I could love someone I hardly even know, that's all.'

Belle looked confused. 'But Fred, there are so many pretty girls in the kingdom. Why shouldn't you fall in love with one of them?'

I sighed. Sometimes I forgot my stepsisters were only eight. They thought love was what they felt when they saw my best friends, Angelo, the fiery-tempered Italian messenger boy, or Matthew, the happy-go-lucky stable hand.

'Because you don't fall in love with someone's face. Looks may be the start of it, but it's really the personality that counts,' I tried to explain.

It didn't work. Belle and Grace looked as confused as ever.

'Okay. Imagine that there are two girls,' I said, trying again, 'and one of them is absolutely drop-dead gorgeous but has no personality, or the personality of a rattlesnake. And the other one is really, well, let's say, un-pretty, but has as much sparkle as a bottle of wine, as much personality as ... as you two. Who do you think will end up getting more dates?'

Belle and Grace looked at each other, still confused.

'The ... the pretty one?' guessed Belle, unsure.

I slapped my forehead, and shook my head. 'Well, at first, yeah. But then, as people get to know them both, they'll realise that the other girl is a lot more fun to be with. And in the end, you

can bet she'll be the one beating guys off with sticks.'

Belle smiled.

'So ugly people are more fun?' she said, thinking she understood what I had said completely.

I shook my head, and it took me about another fifty minutes to finally explain to them what I meant.

'What time is it?' I asked eventually.

Belle looked at me and shrugged.

'I dunno.'

I sat down on my chair again, and then jumped back up when I heard horses' hooves clattering up the path to the castle's main entrance.

'Well, I've got to go. Wish me luck, okay?' I said as I left the room.

Not that any amount of luck is going to help me fall in love tonight, I added silently.

3

The ball got into full swing and, as I had expected, I didn't feel the slightest romantic twinge for any of the 'young ladies'. Some of the girls that I knew, like Beth and Maria, didn't actually care about romance. They had just come because they were invited. And that was fine by me because I didn't want them as anything other than good friends, which was what they were. The other girls were practically throwing themselves at me. There were two in particular who agreed with everything I said, liked everything I liked, and told me every bad thing about every other girl there. They were called Priscilla and Rosemary, and, as I found out later, they were sisters. They were also extremely unattractive.

I was in the middle of yet another boring dance with Priscilla when I saw someone standing at the door. She had only just arrived.

I'd danced with everyone else, so I would've remembered her. I mean, I could hardly have forgotten someone like her. She was really beautiful. Her long, soft red hair flowed delicately over her green and cream silk dress and her cheeks had a slight tinge of pink. She looked so lost, I felt I just had to go and dance with her (what did I have to lose anyway?).

As I looked around the ballroom, I saw that I wasn't the only one who had noticed the late arrival. Angelo and Matthew had also seen her, and were already making their way across the ballroom to her. 'Um, excuse me, Priscilla,' I said, pushing myself away from her. Actually, I was glad of any excuse to get away from her. I quickened my pace, but I was too late. Angelo had already won the first dance. Matthew was leaning against the wall and staring at Angelo with venom as he led the mystery girl onto the dance floor.

I say mystery, and she was definitely one. I had never seen her before, and that really is surprising since I'd been all around the kingdom in the eighteen years I'd been a prince, and I thought I'd seen everyone.

'What'd he do?' I asked Matthew as I joined him. 'Hit her with one of his *amazing* chat-up lines, or feed her a load of romantic Italian rubbish that no one ever understands anyway?'

Matthew ran his fingers through his fair hair and shook his head. 'Neither. He just asked her to dance,' he replied in amazement.

We watched for a few minutes, and when the band started to play a new piece of music, Angelo and Miss Mystery returned.

'Hey, Frederico. How's the birthday boy?' asked Angelo, leaning against the wall.

I smiled.

'Oh, I'm absolutely wonderful,' I said sarcastically.

We talked for a little while and then, when the next song was being played, I made my move. Unfortunately, so did Angelo and Matthew.

'Do you want to dance?' (That was Matthew)

'Would you like to dance?' (That was me)

'How about another dance?' (Work it out for yourself!)

She laughed, and I noticed that her laugh sounded like the gentle tinkling of silver bells, and when her brown eyes sparkled, they looked like dark amber jewels.

'I think I owe this one to the person who's hosting the ball, don't you?'

'Yeah, whatever,' grumbled Angelo.

'Thanks a lot, Fred,' moaned Matthew.

'Don't worry,' I called to them, as I led the way to the dance floor, 'you can always get Priscilla and Rosemary to dance with you.'

I looked at the clock. It was only eleven, and the ball would continue until at least six in the morning. That gave us plenty of time to get to know each other. So, what first? Say something, Fred, something ... anything. Just talk to her.

'I, um, I like your dress,' I said, and immediately felt like kicking myself.

I like your dress? What sort of an idiot was she going to think I was?

'Thanks, it's new,' was her only response.

Phew!

Wait a minute! Did she say new?

UH OH!

I must have danced with a hundred girls wearing new dresses, and most of them were nearly as bad as Priscilla or Rosemary. Okay, Fred, don't worry. Maybe it wasn't that expensive.

'It must have cost a lot,' I said, crossing my fingers behind her back.

She shook her head, and her hair bounced

gently against my hand.

'No, it didn't. My ... my godmother made it for me,' she replied.

Oh, okay. That's fine. No problems there.

'Is she a tailor?' I asked, glad she'd brought up another subject we could talk about.

'She's a ... woman of many talents,' she said, as she looked rather nervously at the clock on the wall.

'What else does she do?' I asked her.

'Stuff you wouldn't believe,' she replied with a grin.

Oh yeah? Like what? Grant wishes?

As we danced and talked, I found myself liking her more and more. She had all the qualities that Beth and Maria had. She was understanding, she was an individual and she was really funny. But there was something else about her too. Something that made me want her as more than just a friend.

We had quite a lot in common. We were both eighteen years old, but she was a few weeks older than me. Both our mothers were dead, but hers had died when she was eight years old.

Both our fathers had remarried, mine when I was thirteen years old, hers when she was ten years old. As a result of the marriages, we each had two stepsisters. But while Dad had married a widowed kitchen-maid with twin daughters who were younger than me, her father had married a rich widow who had two daughters who were both older than her. The one thing we didn't have in common was that her father had died when she was twelve years old, leaving her to live with her stepmother and stepsisters.

I had finally decided I liked her best and I was about to ask her name, when suddenly the clock rang the first stroke of twelve. DONG!

Without a word, she pulled away from me and ran to the door. I ran after her, but as the second bell rang, she was already outside and running to the steps. DONG!!

As I reached the top of the steps, she was at the bottom. DONG!!!

I ran down the steps towards her, but she was in her carriage by the fourth bell. DONG!!!!

The next eight bells saw her being driven down the path and out of sight, and saw me reaching the bottom of the steps and watching in dismay as she disappeared into the distance.

Both anger and heartbreak welled up inside my chest and I kicked my way up the steps, with my head down. It was a good thing that I did keep my head down, because if I hadn't, I might never have seen her delicate glass slipper lying on the seventh step. I bent down and picked it up. I decided to keep it, to remind me of her.

4

I stamped up the steps and into the ballroom. I didn't feel much like dancing, but I had to go through the ballroom to get to my bedroom.

I stormed upstairs, kicking each step hard. I stamped past the spare dining room where the twins and their friends were hard at work demolishing my trifles and cakes. After a series of twists and turns which I knew inside out (I'd lived in the castle my whole life and could have found my way around it blind-folded), I reached my bedroom. I stomped inside and slammed the door shut. I threw the glass slipper on my bed, and then grabbed a book off my table. I opened

it and looked at the words written on the first page:

To Prince Fred "The Charming" (nice name.)

Happy 18th birthday and good luck at the ball. Don't worry, some day your Princess will come.

Love from King Charming and Queen Snow White

Tales of the Vertically Challenged
by Sleepy & Assoc.

Some day my princess would come! Yeah, right! What would they know? Snow White was dead when they met. Choked to death on a poisoned apple while living with seven short guys. Sounds like one of those bedtime stories. I ripped the page out angrily, scrunched it into a ball and threw it in the bin. Then I flung the book across the room. True love! Who needed it anyway?

The door opened slowly, and Belle and Grace came in.

'Fred?' said Belle nervously.

I turned around. 'Don't you know how to knock? What do you want?' I shouted.

Belle and Grace looked at me as if no one had ever shouted at them before. Their eyes were full of tears.

'We heard you coming upstairs and we thought that maybe something was wrong,' explained Belle, with tears pouring down her cheeks.

I could have kicked myself. Okay, so my night hadn't exactly gone well. You didn't have to be a wizard to figure that out. But that was no excuse to take it out on everyone else. I mean, I never wanted that ball in the first place, did I? 'I'm sorry. I've had a bit of trouble at the ball,' I apologised. 'I shouldn't have shouted at you.'

Grace smiled. 'That's okay,' she said gently. 'Want to tell us about it?'

I shook my head and looked at the book of fairy tales that King Charming and his wife had

given to me. I remembered what they had written on the first page and suddenly felt angry again.

'No! I don't want to tell you. But I will tell you something,' I said angrily, hoping they could tell I wasn't angry at *them*. 'Don't believe what you read in those stupid bedtime fairy stories. Beautiful girls appearing out of the blue, winning the prince's heart and living happily ever after. It just doesn't happen in real life.'

Belle smiled. 'So it's girl trouble then?' she asked.

Was it that obvious? I nodded.

'Maybe we could help?' she suggested.

'I don't think so,' I replied gratefully.

'It wouldn't hurt to tell us,' insisted Grace.

'Well,' I said thoughtfully, 'I don't ... okay. You might even be some help ... for once!'

Belle and Grace looked at me indignantly, but smiled.

'Is that her slipper?' asked Grace when I was finished. 'It's tiny. I don't even wear a shoe that size, and I'm only eight.'

Belle picked the slipper up and looked at it.

'I'll bet she's the only girl her age in the kingdom who wears shoes that size,' she remarked, and then added suddenly, 'and I bet I know how to find her!'

I looked up. 'How?'

Belle smiled. 'Like I said, she's probably the only girl in the kingdom who's eighteen and has a foot the size of a seven-year-old's. So tomorrow, you and some other guys go around the houses of everyone you invited, and get

them to try the shoe on. She might look completely different, but the shoe is a sure way to find her.'

I hugged her so tight she could barely breathe.

'Belle, you're one of the two most wonderful sisters anyone could ever have,' I said.

I think Grace knew who the other one was.

'By the way, what are you two doing still up?' I asked, suddenly remembering the time.

Belle looked at Grace and smiled. 'Fred, we're having a slumber party,' she said, as though she thought that I was the most stupid person that she had ever met. 'You don't actually expect us to sleep, do you?'

Now, I might be wrong, but I always thought that slumber meant sleep. So I sort of assumed that a slumber party was a party at which you slept. Oh well, I guess I'm getting a bit out of it now that I've legally become an adult.

'Um, no, of course not,' I grinned. 'So, uh, what're you doing anyway?'

Grace shrugged. 'Nothing much. You know, girl-stuff. We're telling ghost stories.'

Girl-stuff. Great. Hate to tell you, Grace, but

I'm not actually a girl and I haven't the slightest
idea what 'girl-stuff' is.

'Okay. Don't bother about locking the door,'
I told them.

Grace looked at me, confused.

'What?' she asked.

I tried to look serious. 'In case of ghosts and
monsters and stuff like that,' I replied. 'I mean
the ones that aren't strong enough to break it
down will probably just slide under it.'

Belle laughed. 'Yeah, right. I'm telling you, it's
a good job you'll be king when you're older.
You'd be hopeless at any other job. You couldn't
sell a dog a pile of bones, and you couldn't lie
to save your life.'

Huh! That's what you think, my darling little
sister.

5

When I got downstairs the party was still in full swing. I headed towards the throne room.

'Uh, Dad,' I said, settling myself in the chair opposite his, 'I've got some good news, some bad news and some more good news.'

My father frowned and folded his arms across his chest. 'What's the good news?' he asked hopefully.

'I've found the girl that I think I could marry!' I told him.

The slightly worried look on Dad's face disappeared and he gave a burst of joyous laughter.

'Ha, ha! I knew you could do it, my son. It's all that wonderful charm that runs in the family. Oh, I wish your mother could be here. Tell me, what's her name?'

'I don't know,' I said quietly.

'That's such a beautiful ...' started my father,

but then his face dropped as he realised what I'd said. 'You don't know? What do you mean, you don't know? Didn't you ask her before you proposed to her?'

I suddenly noticed how interesting the floor was. So interesting I didn't take my eyes off it as I told him: 'Dad, I haven't actually proposed to her yet.'

Dad's face went from slightly worried to pretty upset.

'You haven't proposed to her yet?' he boomed. 'What do you mean you haven't proposed to her yet? Why haven't you proposed to her?'

Gosh, that floor was really fascinating today. 'Well, Dad, that's ... that's the bad news.'

Dad looked at me suspiciously. 'What's the bad news?'

Did I say fascinating? The floor was so amazing that I could have stared at it all through the conversation (and I did for most of it).

'She's ... she's sort of ... em ... she's gone.'

That suspicious, pretty upset face opposite me turned into a very angry, bright red face.

'WHAT DO YOU MEAN, SHE'S GONE? HOW CAN SHE BE GONE? WHERE'S SHE GONE TO? WHAT DID YOU DO TO MAKE HER GONE ... GO?'

Me? What did I do? How could he accuse me? I'd never been accused of anything in my life and I'd certainly never been shouted at! Suddenly I knew how Belle and Grace must have felt when I shouted at them. But at least I had apologised. How many times have you heard a king apologise to anyone? None? That's twice as many times as I have, and I live with one. I must admit that I was close to tears at that moment.

Now, I'm not one of those people who think that it's babyish to cry, but the only time that I've ever cried as far as I can remember was when my mother died, and then I couldn't stop. So for me to be close to tears now must prove to you how much I was used to having everything going my way. But I didn't expect Dad to apologise to me, so I told him what happened at the ball. He didn't say anything, but I could tell that he was sorry and that was enough.

'Dad,' I said, 'I told you there was some more good news, and there is. Belle came up with this brilliant idea.'

I continued to tell him the plan in full detail. 'So I thought that I'd ask Angelo and Matthew to come with me,' I concluded proudly. 'I just have to okay it with you. What do you say, Dad? Can I go tomorrow?'

After the way Dad had carried on when I told him she'd gone, I'd expected him to shake my hand, pat me on the back and say, 'That's my son, never ready to give up. Of course you can go.' So I was completely stunned when he shook his head and answered, 'No! Absolutely not. You know hardly anything about her. She could be a kitchen-maid for all you know!' What? I knew my Dad was a bit of a snob, but this was a bit much, wasn't it?

'Dad, she's not a kitchen-maid. She told me her stepmom was rich. Besides, even if she was a kitchen-maid, what difference would it make?'

My Dad just laughed. 'Son, a prince cannot marry a kitchen-maid,' he replied.

Oh, no?

'Why not?' I asked. 'You did.'

Ha! Answer that one, you snob!

'I was a widower, she was a widow and we both needed a partner to help bring up our children. It was the best thing for you and the twins,' he replied, 'but son, generally, marrying a kitchen maid is not the done thing by royalty.'

Good answer.

But Dad wasn't the only example I had. What about his best friend? 'Didn't King Roland marry a miller's daughter?'

Well? Didn't he?

'Only because he had promised her that if she spun all the straw in that room into gold then he'd marry her.'

Okay, Dad might take a bit more convincing than I had planned, but there was one last chance.

'Dad, the whole point of having this ball was so that I could find a bride. The reason I invited people like Beth, Maria and the others is so that I could get to know a girl who didn't have life handed to her on a silver platter. Someone who had to work to get what went on the dinner table. I didn't want to marry into another royal family and have yet another bunch of blue-blooded kids running through the castle. Besides, now that I'm eighteen, I don't have to ask your consent about anything. You can try and stop me, but it would look better if we worked together to find her.'

The truth was, the king can stop anyone doing

anything if he wants to. I was just hoping Dad wouldn't remember that.

Dad smiled. 'You're right, of course. Okay, son, good luck.'

Huh! And Belle said I couldn't lie to save my life.

I thanked Dad and then headed downstairs to find Angelo and Matthew.

I ran into the ballroom and looked around but I couldn't see Angelo or Matthew anywhere. There was a group of chaperons near the stairs and I decided to ask if any of them knew where my friends were.

'Have any of you seen Angelo or Matthew?' I asked.

They looked at me blankly.

'Who?' asked one of them.

'You know, Angelo Marconi? Italian guy, tall, dark hair.'

That jogged their memories. 'Right! The Italian guy. Yeah, he's over there with the other guy, Matthew Simons.'

'Great, thanks.'

'Hi, guys, can I talk to you?' I asked as I joined them.

Angelo smiled widely. 'Hi, Fred. Hey, where's the mystery girl? If you're not with her, I might grab her for another dance. After I've talked to you, of course.'

I rubbed the back of my neck with my left hand. 'Well, that's sort of what I want to talk to you about,' I said awkwardly.

Matthew looked puzzled. I continued. 'See, she sort of ran off at midnight,' I tried to explain. Matthew and Angelo looked at each other. I told them everything that had happened (my third time that day. I felt sure I'd be saying it in my sleep that night).

'And you want us to come with you?' finished Matthew.

'Right,' I replied. 'Will you?'

Angelo nodded. 'Sure, I've got tomorrow off anyway.'

'How about you, Matt?' I asked.

Matthew shrugged. 'I've got work tomorrow,' he replied.

'Am I the king's son, or what?' I exclaimed. 'If Dad wants me to find a wife, he's gonna have to help, isn't he?'

'YEEEEEEEEES!!!!!!!!!!!!!' yelled Matthew.

The whole ballroom turned around and looked at him. I don't know about you, but if that happened to me I would have been too embarrassed to look at them, let alone talk back. But Matthew just turned around, stared at them and told them, 'I'm used to girls staring at me, but I get worried when the guys stare too.'

6

It took a lot of arranging, and a lot ot work persuading Dad to let Matthew have the day off, but finally we had everything prepared. I could barely sleep that night (okay, fine. If you're gonna be technical, then yes, two a.m. is the morning. But you knew what I meant anyway) because I was so nervous about the next morning, but at last it came.

I got up and dressed and washed quickly. Then I ran downstairs to the dining room. As I rushed through my breakfast, I saw Sandra staring at me.

'Fred,' she said, 'it's not going to run away. Slow down. You'll give yourself a sore stomach.'

I looked at her. 'Sandra, I can't slow down. They're out there by the stables waiting for me. I'm late.'

Sandra rolled her eyes and shook her head. 'Look, you're not getting married. Don't panic.'

I pushed my plate away. 'Well, I can't eat any more. I'm going, okay?'

'No, it's not okay. Finish your breakfast.'

'I don't want to finish my breakfast, I want to go.'

'Not until you've finished your breakfast. Fred, you can't go galloping around the kingdom on an empty stomach. You'll get hungry. I bet Angelo had breakfast.'

At long, long, long last, I finally managed to get down to the stables. Angelo and Matthew were already there, and Matthew had saddled up the horses. 'Hi, Fred!' he greeted me, leading two horses out of the stable. Angelo had a third horse who he was talking to in Italian. 'You can have Misty, okay?'

'Sure. But I thought Misty was your favourite,' I replied, taking Misty's reins.

'Yeah, she is. But I figured she'd be more suitable for you today.'

I frowned, confused. 'How'd you figure that?' I asked, rubbing Misty's nose.

Matt grinned. 'You know, Misty sort of sounds

like Miss Mystery. And since that's who we're looking for I thought that she might bring you luck.'

I smiled.

Matthew looked over at Angelo.

'Tu sei un asino stupido,' Angelo was saying lovingly to the horse.

'Hey, Ang!' called Matthew.

Angelo looked up. 'Yeah?'

Matthew mounted his horse expertly. 'When you're finished telling the horse she's a stupid

donkey, would you care to join us?'

Angelo carefully put his right foot into the left stirrup and pulled himself up until he was sitting neatly on the horse. Backwards!

'Hey!' he exclaimed. 'Where'd his head go?'

Matthew and I looked at each other in despair. 'On the other end,' I told him impatiently.

'Well, what's it doing there?' he asked angrily. 'I told you she was stupid. She doesn't even know what end her head should be on.' As Angelo got off and remounted properly, Matthew turned to me. 'You know, Fred,' he said, making sure Angelo could hear, 'there may be a stupid donkey here, but it's certainly not the horse.' Angelo rode up to us.

'Gee, like, thanks a lot, Matthew,' he said angrily. Matthew grinned.

As we galloped out of the palace grounds, I put the slipper into the saddle-bag. Angelo had the list of houses we had to go to. There were only about thirty altogether, though there had been near to a couple of hundred people in the ballroom last night. I guess when you take into account that there were about three daughters in each house and the occasional cousin staying over for the ball, and when you counted all the guys as well, then there must have been at least that many. There was also the kitchen staff who'd come after work, but I didn't have to check them 'cos I knew them all anyway.

Angelo took out the list as we entered the village. 'Okay, we can rule out Beth,' he said looking at it.

'Yeah, and Maria,' added Matthew.

'That leaves over thirty-four houses to check. We'll be all day,' groaned Angelo. 'On my day off.'

Soon we reached the first house on the list. Matthew jumped off his horse and knocked on the door. A pretty blonde girl opened it.

'May I speak to any young ladies who attended the royal ball last night?' he asked in his most polite tone.

The girl smiled and called her sisters. I knew at once that none of them was the girl I was looking for, but what could I do? I asked them to try on the slipper anyway, although I knew it wouldn't fit. So

I was surprised when I heard the youngest shout as she tried on the slipper, 'IT FITS!'

I spun around to look at her. 'Let's see,' I said.

She lifted up her foot sheepishly. The shoe was hanging off.

'Oops, I guess I made a mistake,' she admitted quietly.

'A mistake. Yeah, right! Give me that!' ordered Angelo, snatching the slipper from her foot.

'The things some people will do!' added Matthew in disgust.

Apparently it wasn't only some people, but most people, who'd stoop to such tricks to get the chance to marry me. But I mean, could you blame them? Who wouldn't want a husband who was tall, dark, handsome, and yet not the least bit vain? Of course, the fact that I was the richest guy in the kingdom, and a prince, might have had a little bit to do with it.

I had started off the day feeling confident and sure that I would find her, but after four hours travelling around the kingdom on horseback, I was becoming pretty depressed. I know some of you probably think that I'm a liar, telling Belle and Grace you can't fall in love at first sight and then going to all this trouble over some girl I only met once. But the truth is, I wasn't in love with her. I just figured I'd talked to all the girls in the kingdom and that out of all of them, she was the one I would be most likely to fall in love with, given time. Remember, I wasn't going crazy about just her looks or anything; they were an added bonus. I'd spent most of the night getting to know her, and I knew she was nice.

As we approached yet another house, I noticed Angelo studying the list hard. 'What's up?' I asked him.

'Uh, Fred, have we been to the terrible twosome's house yet?' he asked me.

I knew he meant Priscilla and Rosemary. I shook my head.

'Oh, 'cos see, this is the last house.'

Matthew and I stopped our horses quickly. 'What?' I asked, sounding like a mouse with a sore throat. 'She can't be related to them.'

Matthew looked at me.

'She could be their cousin,' he suggested, helpfully.

Angelo raised his eyebrows.

'How could she be related to them?' he scorned.

'True,' replied Matt.

Suddenly his face brightened. 'Hey! Maybe she gatecrashed!'

Angelo rolled his eyes. 'And you call me stupid?' he laughed. 'How exactly do you gatecrash the prince's ball? I mean, there was more security there than in the king's royal mint, and no one's ever broken in there before. Gatecrashing the prince's party, what next? Frogs that turn into princes, Goldilocks?'

Matthew ran his fingers through his fair hair. 'It was just a suggestion,' he said.

I sighed and turned my horse towards the last house. 'Come on,' I said. 'We might as well give it a try. They *might* know her.'

Slowly, we rode up to the door. I dismounted and lifted my hand to knock, but the door flew open. 'PRINCEY!' cried Rosemary, and she hugged me so tight I started to turn purple.

As I tried to struggle free, Matthew and Angelo got down. Angelo took the slipper from my saddle-bag.

'Rosemary, let go of the prince,' he said, coming over.

'But it's my Princey, and he's come to ask me to marry him,' she answered in a disgustingly squeaky voice.

'Well, he won't be marrying anyone if you don't let him go,' Matthew told her.

Slowly, Rosemary let me go.

'Actually,' said Angelo, 'he wants anyone who was at the ball last night to try on this shoe.'

Rosemary turned around. 'PRISCILLA,' she shrieked, 'PRINCE CHARMING'S HERE.'

Priscilla came running out of the house, wobbling in ten different directions as she did.

'Look,' said Angelo quickly, 'could you just try on this slipper? If it fits you, you can marry him.'

Suddenly, a tall, skinny, cruel-looking woman appeared at the door.

'Well, Prince Charming. This *is* a surprise,' she said.

For some reason, her voice sent a chill down

my back. 'Why don't you and your friends come in?'

Angelo and I looked at each other.

'Well, just for a minute. Then I'd better be getting back to the palace,' I replied.

'Guess what, Mother?' screeched Priscilla. 'He might be marrying one of us.'

Her mother smiled a strange smile. 'That would be pleasant, wouldn't it, my prince?' she said in an icy tone.

'Uh, yes, quite,' I answered. I was scared of her. There was something about her which I couldn't place, but it frightened me.

'Why don't you just try on the shoe?' suggested Matthew to Rosemary.

And get it over with, I added silently.

'I'll have no trouble fitting *my* shoe on my foot,' she said, sitting down.

She took off a black boot to reveal the biggest foot I had ever seen. A smell of rotten cabbages filled the room.

'Here,' said Angelo, handing her the shoe.

I nearly laughed when I saw big-footed Rosemary trying to shove her foot into a shoe half its size.

'I told you it would fit,' she said at last. Matthew yawned. Yet another stupid trick.

'Show me your foot,' he said boredly.

Rosemary slowly lifted her foot to show that all her toes were sticking out of the top of her shoe. There wasn't much difference when Priscilla tried on the shoe. We were just about to go when I heard a voice behind me.

7

'Stepmother, I've got the tea.'

I spun around.

'Cinderella, go back to the kitchen!' hollered her stepmother.

'No, wait,' I said.

I couldn't believe my eyes, and neither could Angelo or Matthew, judging by the looks on their faces.

She was dressed in rags, her face was dirty and her hair was tied back, but it was definitely her. Miss Mystery. 'Um ... would you try on this slipper, please?' I asked, unable to believe it was her.

'I ....' she started.

'Oh, you needn't bother with her. She's just a kitchen-maid,' her stepmother told me.

'I want her to try on the slipper,' I told her firmly.

Angelo smiled and tossed the slipper in the

air. Then he put his hand out and caught it skilfully, much to my relief.

'Had you worried, did I Fred? Well, don't worry. I'm being careful,' he assured me. 'We'd be lost without this thing. Speaking of which ....'

Cinderella sat down on a chair nearby. She didn't have any shoes to take off, but her bare feet were the only ones that would fit the slipper.

Angelo started to walk over to her with the slipper, but Cindy's stepmother stretched out her foot. Angelo didn't notice until it was too late. He crashed to the ground and the glass slipper was shattered into about a hundred and twenty pieces.

'Oh, you poor boy!' cried Cindy's stepmother as she rushed over. She grabbed his arm to help him up. I don't know who she thought her concerned act would fool, but it sure didn't fool Angelo.

'Don't touch me. Do you think I'm stupid? You tripped me and ruined my best friend's chance of happiness. Thanks a lot.'

Quietly, Cindy spoke from the corner. 'Perhaps I could help?' she suggested, and before anyone said anything, she took the other

slipper from her pocket.

Slowly, Angelo walked over and, taking the shoe from her hand, slipped it onto her foot.

'Well, what do you know!' he announced. 'It fits.'

Suddenly there was a flash of light and a weird-looking lady with wings and a magic wand appeared behind Cindy.

'Uh, Cinderella, not meaning to be nosy or anything, but who's that lady behind you with the wings?' I asked.

Cinderella turned around. 'Oh,' she said in surprise as she gave the lady a hug. 'Fred, this is my ... godmother, who made the dress.'

I glanced at Angelo and Matthew, who looked as amazed as I felt.

'Your ... your *godmother*?' I repeated.

'My Fairy Godmother.'

Whoa, I was joking when I said she granted wishes!

Cindy's stepmother and stepsisters were thrown out of the house, which had been left to Cindy in her father's will, as soon as I told my father what had happened. They moved to another kingdom, far away from mine. I kept seeing Cinderella, of course, and I married her the day after my nineteenth birthday.

I actually convinced my Dad to call me Fred, instead of son, but he still hates it.

Matthew got promoted to head groom, and he married Angelo's cousin, Maria the same day I got married.

Actually, it was a triple wedding, because Angelo finally proposed to Beth. He's not a messenger boy any more. I appointed him as my official bodyguard. He's been taking boxing lessons since he was six, and he has trouble finding sparring partners. That's how good he is.

Belle and Grace are dating Matthew's and Angelo's brothers, Peter and Mario. Could there be marriage on the cards there? I don't know, but with a bit of luck, we'll all live happily ever after.

THE END